Moon Watchers

SHIRIN'S RAMADAN MIRACLE

Reza Jalali

Illustrated by
Anne Sibley O'Brien

TILBURY HOUSE PUBLISHERS, THOMASTON, MAINE

J lean up against my father as the sky gets darker around us. Way above our heads, tiny stars start to appear. We search for the new moon. I hear the back door open.

"Moon Watchers," Mom calls. "Come inside if you're done. Dinner is ready."

We make our way back in the dark and take off our shoes before entering the bright house. The room is filled with the smell of rice, fried eggplant, and potatoes.

"Is the new moon out?" Maman-Bozorg asks. She is my grandmother.

"Not yet, but maybe later tonight Ramadan will begin," Dad says and heads for the sink to wash his hands.

"Shirin, would you please go tell your brother the food is ready?" Mom asks. I find Ali playing a video game. I tell him it's time to eat.

"Wait," he says without looking at me.

"Wait," I mumble, mocking him.

"I heard that," Ali says, glaring at me.

"Mom wants you to stop the game right now," I say and walk away, feeling good to have the last word.

I ask my grandmother to tell me more about Ramadan.

"You know that Ramadan starts with the sighting of the new moon," she begins. "Muslims use the lunar calendar. This is a holy month to pray more, to help others, and to be an especially good person."

"We go without food and water during the daylight hours of the month," Dad adds. "Fasting teaches us what it means to be hungry, to be thankful for what we have."

I chew on the crispy rice from the bottom of the pot. It's delicious.

"So when exactly does the fasting start?" I ask, looking up from my plate.

"Don't talk with your mouth full," Ali says. He always treats me like a child, even though he is only three years older than I am.

"We begin once we see the new moon," Dad says.

"Is it hard to go without anything to eat or drink for the whole day?" I ask.

"For you it would be," Ali jumps in.

"Shirin's only nine," Mom says, looking at Ali.

Feeling adventurous, I ask, "Can I fast this Ramadan?"

"You're too young, my daughter." Dad pats my head as if I am Pishi, our cat!

"You have to wait till you get to be my age," Ali says.

"If he fasts, you have to let me," I insist.

"You are too young," Ali says.

"No, I am not."

"Please stop that," Mom says with a sigh. She hates it when we argue.

After dinner, Dad and I go outside to continue our sky gazing.

"There it is!" he says. He sounds excited, but I can't see anything. Dad kneels down and points his finger at the top of the trees.

"Keep looking at the middle of the pine," he says. Then I see a thin, pale crescent hidden in the branches. It looks like the ghost of a little bird.

"That's the new moon?" I had expected a big, shiny, round thing.

"Yes, it is. Ramadan is here," Dad says. "Let's go inside to tell everyone."

I watch the light dance wildly over the grass as we walk back.
Pishi chases the yellow beam. It still bothers me that Ali gets to fast.

"Won't you let me fast, just for a few days?" I tug at Dad's sleeve.

"Shirin, you're too young, but remember there's more to Ramadan
than fasting. Why don't you think of some good deeds to help others
in our family? You could help take care of Pishi or weed in the garden."

*I*nside, my family gets ready to pray. Dad spreads a colorful prayer mat on the soft carpet and places the heart-shaped prayer stone on it. He stands straight, with his eyes closed and his lips moving.

I want to join in the prayers, so I run to my room for the special scarf Maman-Bozorg gave me. It is dark blue, with beads. I throw it on the carpet next to Dad's mat. I watch him from the corner of my eye to copy him.

Together we stand, bow, kneel, and press our foreheads to the floor. Then we get up and do the same moves again. In the end, my father bows and murmurs words in the direction of the open window. He brings his face to the floor, his forehead touching the prayer stone, and kisses it three times.

Dad turns to me. "Shirin, ask Allah for something!" With eyes shut, I pray for straighter hair and better grades. When I open my eyes, I see him smiling at me.

*I*n the morning, I am the only one having breakfast. Maman-Bozorg is still in bed. Mom is helping Ali get ready for school. Except for the ticktock of the wall clock, the house is quiet. The samovar sits on the cold stove. I miss the sound of its hissing as it brings water to a boil for tea.

"Remember to drink water if you have to," Mom says to Ali.

"I'll be fine, Mom," he replies and looks at me. "This isn't the first time I've fasted."

I feel jealous and stop eating my cereal. "Why can't I fast?"

"You think you could manage without food for the whole day?" Ali asks with a smirk as he heads for the door.

When I get home from school, Mom looks pale.

"Are you hungry?" I ask her.

"Just tired," she says.

"How much longer before you are allowed to eat?"

"Not until after the sun goes down, but I'm making dinner for you now."

By the time Dad comes home, it's nearly dark.

"Is it almost time to break the fast?" I ask.

"It's called iftar," Ali corrects me.

Mom is busy cooking. The water is boiling for tea and there are small dishes of sweets on the counter.

"Shirin, you can eat again with us if you want," Mom says. She hands me a bowl of steaming bean soup.

"May Allah feed whoever is hungry," Maman-Bozorg says before drinking her first glass of tea. Dad pours some milk for Ali.

"Do you want to have dates with your milk?" Mom asks Ali. He nods his head and smiles.

"Can I have some dates, too?" I ask.

"Absolutely."

After we finish eating, it's time to pray again. Maman-Bozorg
and Mom wear their chadors. As Mom stands and sits, the
soft cloth catches the breeze. She looks beautiful.

Later, I ask, "How come you don't always wear a scarf
like Maman-Bozorg?"

Mom laughs and says, "You know, not every Muslim
woman covers her hair."

"But in the pictures Auntie sends us she always wears a scarf."

"In her country it is the custom. There are different traditions about such things. But all Muslims use the same prayers and we all observe Ramadan."

"I still want to fast."

Maman-Bozorg looks up from her prayer mat. "Shirin, I have been thinking about your desire to be part of Ramadan. Have you thought of doing some good deeds?" she asks softly.

"Yes, but I'm still trying to figure out what to do," I answer. I only know that I want to do something that will surprise my family.

In the days that follow, everyone continues to fast—except me. Sometimes during the night I wake up and listen to the sounds of their voices as they eat.

Dad and I still go out for our moon watching. As the nights go by, the moon slowly gets bigger and brighter.

"The moon is getting fatter," I say one evening, standing outside with Dad. Pishi is looking up at the silvery half-moon, too. She arches her back and runs away to vanish in the darkness beyond the trees.

Dad says, "The moon changes its shape as Ramadan moves on."

"I like it when it gets to be really big again," I say.

"Soon it will be a full moon, and we will be halfway through Ramadan," Dad tells me.

A few days later, Dad teases Mom as she complains of headaches.

"Admit it. You miss your morning tea!"

"Maybe," she says, and winks at me. "But I don't see you playing tag with your daughter as usual."

I jump up, saying, "Come on, Dad, come get me!"

He just sits there and looks serious. I miss Dad chasing me from room to room. I love it when he catches me and lifts me over his head and pretends to drop me down. I ask him if he will pick me up.

He shakes his head. "You're a big girl now."

"Then why don't you let me fast?" I beg once again.

"You have to be patient and wait a year or two," he says.

"Shirin, let me tell you a story," Maman-Bozorg says with a mysterious smile.

"Yeki bood, yeki nabood," she starts.

"Once upon a time…." In my head, I translate the words into English.

"There was a small boy who wanted to fast for Ramadan like the elders in the family. He kept asking his parents to let him do so. His mother came up with a clever compromise. She said, 'What if you were to fast in bits and pieces for parts of the day?'"

Dad sips his tea and watches my grandmother as she fixes her scarf and continues.

"'Would Allah accept my fasting even though it is only done part time?' the small boy asked.

"'Of course Allah would like such an offering!' the mother said. 'Your part-time fasting would be beautiful and precious—the way a quilt is beautiful—all different pieces becoming one gift.' The boy liked the plan. So from that day on, he kept his part-time fast during Ramadan and everyone was happy. The end," Maman-Bozorg says, finishing her story.

"Do you know the boy in the story?" I ask, but I know from the way she and my father exchange smiles that my dad was the boy in the tale.

By the next night, the moon is completely round. I go out to the pond in back of our house and see the moon's trembling reflection in the water. When Pishi dips her paw in the pond, the moon breaks into hundreds of tiny silvery pieces. It's so beautiful!

After prayers are done that evening, I ask Dad if I can fast the same way as the boy in Maman-Bozorg's story. He asks Mom what she thinks, and she smiles, looking at me.

"Yes, and I think I will make a quilt myself," she says. "I need something to do to distract me from my longing for tea," she adds, laughing. I go to bed feeling happy to have permission to fast, even if it is only part time!

The next day, when Dad comes home from work, he asks if I'm okay going without breakfast and lunch. He kisses me on my forehead three times, the way he kisses the heart-shaped prayer stone. We go outside to watch the sunset. The sky turns red as if it's on fire. Then, as the darkness of night grows, Dad starts the grill to barbecue chicken. I head inside to help Mom.

"Can you please start the water boiling for tea?" she asks as she drains the water from the rice she is cooking.

"How come Ali does nothing?" I ask.

"He feels too weak," my grandmother says with a little twinkle. "Not everyone fasting is doing as well as you, Shirin." This makes me feel good. I offer to help my mother pin together the squares for the quilt later.

After school the next day, I'm so hungry I could eat a horse! When I open the door to the kitchen, I see Ali stuffing something in his mouth. I almost yell that he is cheating, but I stop. He might have forgotten he is fasting. I know for myself how hard it is to fast. My mouth waters as I watch him take big bites of golden apple.

"What are you doing here?" Ali asks with surprise.

"Nothing," I say. I want to say that I saw him eating. My brother is so sneaky—I want to tell our parents he has broken his fast. But I decide to stay quiet. I think maybe this silence is my first good deed for Ramadan. Ali stares at me. I walk away feeling proud of myself. Maybe Ali will stop teasing me now.

*S*oon the moon starts to get thinner again. It looks like a half-eaten piece of yellow cheese.

"Like me, it is losing weight," my dad jokes. I notice Dad's belly is shrinking.

In the kitchen, Maman-Bozorg is boiling rice in a large pot. I tell her how much I like the special sweet dish she is making.

"When he was a child, your father liked it, too." She lets the rice cook till it gets soggy. She adds lots of sugar and a tiny amount of saffron and leaves it to simmer. Once it cools down, she serves me some.

"I love Ramadan," I say between spoonfuls of the sweet yellow rice. My part-time fast makes all this food taste even better than usual.

After being hidden behind the clouds for a few nights in a row, the moon disappears altogether.

"Now we have to wait for the new moon," Dad says. "Once we see it in the sky, Ramadan will be over."

I am excited, because once Ramadan ends, it will be Eid, and there will be presents for Ali and me.

"Do I get more gifts this Eid?" I ask.

"And why would that be?" Dad says.

"Because this Ramadan I have been fasting part time," I say proudly.

The next afternoon, I walk through the kitchen door and see Ali eating—again!
I try to find words that will encourage his fasting, but I hear Mom's footsteps coming
toward us. Ali has left the open cracker box sitting on the counter. I quickly reach out
and put the box back in the cupboard. That's the second good deed I've done for Ali
this Ramadan. Ali looks at me in total surprise. I give him a big wink.

"Kids, what are you doing in the kitchen?" Mom calls.

"Nothing," I answer.

Mom walks in carrying some beautiful squares for the quilt. Ali swallows the crackers
and turns around with a funny look on his face. He knows I've done him a big favor.

"Shirin, come help with the quilt—it's almost finished." I follow her out of the
kitchen.

Later that evening, Dad and I keep up our moon watching. Tonight Ali comes out with us.

After looking for the new moon the next night, Dad rushes inside and says, "The moon watchers have sighted the new moon!" He is exaggerating his voice and sounds like a TV announcer. "Eid ul-Fitr, the time of festivity, is here!"

I feel excited—butterflies in my stomach. I know this Eid is going to be wonderful. But I know that I will also miss the fasting and moon watching of Ramadan.

The next day, Mom says we are going to decorate our hands with henna. "Ramadan spa," she whispers with a big smile. We mix the copper-colored powder with water to make a dark-red paste. Dipping into the mix with a matchstick, Mom paints swirls, dots, and stars on my palms.

I sit on the sofa keeping my hands still, waiting for the henna to dry. Once it dries, the curly lines and the flowers and dots come to life. My palms look like tiny red carpets!

"Put those pretty hands to work here," Mom says, and puts a tray full of dates on the counter. I carefully remove the moist pits so that each date can be stuffed with chopped walnuts.

"Don't eat too many," she says. "I'm making other things, too."

"When will we open our presents?" I ask.

"How about right now?" I hear a voice behind me. I turn to see Ali standing by the door holding a large box.

"I have a gift for my sister who is old enough to fast." He quickly drops the present on the counter and rushes out. Mom looks at me. The confusion on her face matches mine. I lift the gift-wrapped box and shake it a few times.

"Tell me, what is going on?" Mom asks. "Ali is getting you a present on his own?"

I shrug.

"Ramadan miracle?" Mom asks.

"Ramadan miracle," I giggle, smiling back at her.

Author's Note

My family's long-ago Ramadan observances are among my happiest memories of childhood in the Middle East. I recall with fondness those Ramadans of the distant past in Iran, in a faraway town lost to a war that few now remember. Known as "the month of blessing," Ramadan was (and is) a time of prayer, fasting, and charity for Muslims throughout the world. Fasting is practiced to build awareness of the poor and to develop self-discipline. During the daylight hours of Ramadan, Muslims who are old enough refrain from all eating and drinking—including water.

A sense of exhilaration would fill the air on a Ramadan morning. Work hours were flexible during the holy month, but most adults would arise before dawn to eat their pre-fast meal (*suhoor*) before daylight. No leftover food would be served, for traditional and elaborate dishes special to Ramadan were made for the family. Elders would recite verses from the Qur'an, as tradition called for the Holy Book to be read sura by sura, chapter by chapter, throughout the month. We children were too young to fast, but we woke up to share in the revered occasion, knowing that hours later a breakfast would be served to us, prepared by adults who were themselves fasting.

Back then, in bigger cities in Iran, the signal to stop eating and start the fast would be announced by the boom of a single cannon. In smaller towns like ours, before the age of alarm clocks and radios, volunteers moved swiftly through the narrow, winding lanes of neighborhoods, between houses that seemed to lean on each other as if taking a nap, beating the ground and the outside walls with long sticks to wake up the households. Out of respect, they'd avoid houses belonging to the town's non-Muslim residents—Jewish, Armenian, Assyrian, and Yezidi households—or those too old or ill to fast.

At the end of each day, family and friends would gather to share the post-fast evening meal, or *iftar,* which is eaten after sunset. My mother, always the storyteller, told me that in the old days, before the arrival of electricity, those fasting would check the time in the evening by carrying two strings of cloth outdoors—one black, another white—to see if they could be told apart in the waning light. When they looked the same, it was time to break the fast.

Islam uses a lunar calendar (based on the cycles of the moon), and Ramadan always begins on the first night of the new moon in the ninth month of the Islamic year. Because the lunar calendar is shorter than the solar calendar, Ramadan "travels" through the seasons as the years go by. When Ramadan arrives in winter, fasting through the short daylight hours is not quite so much a challenge as it is during long, hot summer days.

Perhaps in part because of childhood Ramadans, I have been a sky watcher all my life. I like the mystery and the majesty of a clear, star-pinned sky. I imagine the millions of others, young and old, near and far, who might look up to watch the same sky and the same twinkling stars that I am seeing. I was a moon watcher as a child, fascinated by how the moon seemed to follow me around. (Afraid of being teased by older boys, I kept this to myself.) Even now, as I walk outside under a full moon in the Maine night sky, I chuckle when I catch a glimpse of the moon following me around.

Ramadan is as important to Muslims as Christmas and Easter are to Christians and Passover, Yom Kippur, and Rosh Hashanah are to Jews. Ramadan ends with the festival of Eid ul-Fitr, which means "Festival of Breaking the Fast." This is a joyous time when friends and family gather and celebrate.

I hope our children, Azad and Setareh, will have their own stories of Ramadan and will share them with others one day. I always wonder what their stories might be about.

Tilbury House Publishers
12 Starr Street
Thomaston, ME 04861
(800) 582-1899
www.tilburyhouse.com

First hardcover edition: May 2010
First paperback edition: May 2017
10 9 8 7 6 5 4 3 2

*For Azad and Setareh, hoping they'll grow to be wise and old to share their own
stories of Ramadan with others. —RJ*

*For Setareh, Azad, Jaleh, and Reza, with thanks for all your gracious assistance.
And with thanks to Charles Wright. —ASOB*

Library of Congress Cataloging-in-Publication Data
Jalali, Reza.
    Moon watchers : Shirin's Ramadan miracle / Reza Jalali ; illustrated by
Anne Sibley O'Brien. — 1st hardcover ed.
        p. cm.
    Summary: Nine-year-old Shirin wants to join her family and other
Muslims in fasting for Ramadan but is told she is too young, and so she
seeks other ways to participate including, perhaps, getting along better
with her older brother, Ali.
    ISBN 978-0-88448-321-2 (hardcover)
    [1. Ramadan.—Fiction. 2. Muslims—Fiction. 3. Islam—Customs
and practices—Fiction. 4. Fasts and feasts—Islam—Fiction. 5. Brothers
and sisters—Fiction. 6. Family life—Fiction.] I. O'Brien, Anne Sibley,
ill. II. Title.
    PZ7.J153557Moo 2010
    [E]—dc22   2009046324

Designed by Geraldine Millham, Westport, Massachusetts.
Printed in South Korea

RELATED BOOKS

Tilbury House publishes award-winning picture books that take children around the world to explore vibrant cultures and ways of life, including:

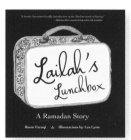

LAILAH'S LUNCHBOX
A Ramadan Miracle
Reem Faruqi
Illustrated by Lea Lyon

Experiencing her first Ramadan in her adopted country of America, Lailah is afraid that her fasting will isolate her from her classmates. The solution reassures her that she can make new friends who respect her beliefs.

Hardcover $16.95 • 978-0-88448-431-8

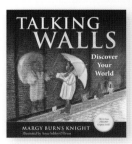

TALKING WALLS
Discover Your World
Margy Burns Knight
Illustrated by Anne Sibley O'Brien

If the Vietnam Memorial, the Great Wall of China, the Western Wall, and other famous walls around the world could talk, what could they tell us? In this book that has sold more than 200,000 copies, walls really do talk, and oh, the stories they tell.

Paperback $9.95 • 978-0-88448-363-2

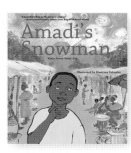

AMADI'S SNOWMAN
Katia Novet Saint-Lot
Illustrated by Dimitrea Tokumbo

Amadi plans to be a great African trader, so why should he learn to read? But a snowman pictured in a book in his village marketplace opens his eyes to a world of possibilities in this tribute to the power of reading.

Paperback $7.95 • 978-0-88448-440-0

MELENA'S JUBILEE
The Story of a Fresh Start
Zetta Elliott
Illustrated by Aaron Boyd

Upon being granted a fresh start by her mother and grandmother after a hard day, Melena resolves to forgive others as she has been forgiven, and she embraces the concept of a jubilee day for the forgiveness of debts and wrongs.

Hardcover $16.95 • 978-0-88448-443-1

THANKS TO THE ANIMALS
Allen Sockabasin
Illustrated by Rebekah Raye

In this gentle, moving story from a master Native American storyteller, little Zoo Sap and his family are moving from their summer home on the Maine coast to their winter home in the deep woods. Unnoticed, the youngster tumbles off the end of the sled. Cold and frightened, he is rescued by the animals of the forest, who keep him safe until his father returns to find him.

Hardcover $17.95 • 978-0-88448-414-1

PASS THE PANDOWDY, PLEASE
Chewing on History with Famous Folks and Their Fabulous Foods
Abigail Ewing Zelz
Illustrated by Eric Zelz

Just like us, the great movers and shakers of history had to eat, and in this colorful, whimsical history book, their favorite foods turn out to be a highly entertaining thread to follow through the history of our small planet.

Hardcover $17.95 • 978-0-88448-468-4

MOST PEOPLE
Michael Leannah
Illustrated by Jennifer Morris

"Most people love to smile. Most people love to laugh. Most people love to see other people smile and laugh too. Most people are good people." This book's reassuring message is always welcome and timely.

Hardcover $16.95 • 978-0-88448-554-4

REZA JALALI is a teacher, writer, and community organizer. Originally from Iran, he has lived in Maine for over two decades. When not working at the University of Southern Maine or playing soccer for fun, he writes stories to delight his children. A sky watcher, he believes we each have a star named after us, and he continues to search the night sky to find his and those of his family and friends.

ANNE SIBLEY O'BRIEN has illustrated 31 books and is the author and illustrator of the picture book *I'm New Here* and the graphic novel *The Legend of Hong Kil Dong*. Annie's passion for multiracial, multicultural, and global subjects grew out of her experience of being raised bilingual and bicultural in South Korea as the daughter of medical missionaries. She writes the column "The Illustrator's Perspective" for the *Bulletin of the Society of Children's Book Writers and Illustrators* and a blog, "Coloring Between the Lines."